How Ganesh Got His Elephant Head

HARISH JOHARI AND VATSALA SPERLING
Illustrated by Pieter Weltevrede

Bear Cub Books
Rochester, Vermont

For Dada

*Special thanks to Sapna Johari for her expert
help in researching the story.*

Bear Cub Books
One Park Street
Rochester, Vermont 05767
www.InnerTraditions.com

Bear Cub Books is a division of Inner Traditions International

Library of Congress Cataloging-in-Publication Data

Johari, Harish.
How Ganesh got his elephant head / Harish Johari, Vatsala
Sperling ; illustrated by Pieter Weltevrede.
p. cm.
Summary: Relates adventures of Ganesh, the Hindu god of prosperity, and
how he became the gods' gift to humanity.
ISBN 1-59143-021-6
1. Gaòneâsa (Hindu deity)—Juvenile literature. [1. Ganesha (Hindu
deity) 2. Mythology, Hindu.] I. Johari, Harish, 1934- II. Sperling,
Vatsala, 1961- III. Weltevrede, Pieter, ill. IV. Title.
BL1225.G34T56 2003
294.5'2113—dc22
2003011307

Printed and bound in India by Replika Press

10 9 8 7 6 5 4 3 2

Text design and layout by Mary Anne Hurhula
This book was typeset in Berkeley with Abbess as the display typeface

Cast of Characters

Brahma
(Brahm-'ha)
God of Creation

Indra
('In-dra)
King of the lesser gods,
ruler of rain and storms

Vishnu
('Vish-noo)
God of Preservation

Kartikeya
(Kar-ti-'kay-a)
Brother of Ganesh,
leader of Indra's army

Shiva
(Shee-'va)
God of Destruction,
husband of Parvati, father
of Ganesh and Kartikeya

Garuda
(Gar-oo-'da)
Vishnu's eagle

Parvati
('Par-va-tee)
A great mother goddess,
wife of Shiva, mother of
Ganesh and Kartikeya

Nav Durga
(Nahv 'Door-ga)
A fierce goddess who
appears in nine forms
and protects against
injustice

Shivaganas
(Shee-va-g'-'nas)
Shiva's assistants, a band
of troublemakers

Kali
(Kah-lee)
The goddess
of destruction

Nandi
(Nahn-dee)
Shiva's pet bull

Saint Narada
('Nah-rah-da)
A holy spirit

Ganesh
(G'-nesh)
The elephant-headed god
who can make things
go right, son of Parvati
and Shiva

This is the story of Ganesh, a very odd-looking and wonderful god. If you were to visit India, you would be sure to see countless little roadside temples built for him in every village and town. And in those temples you would find bowls of sugarcane, fruit, milk, peanuts, and coconuts—and, perhaps, some nice, freshly cut hay! For Ganesh has the body of a chubby little boy, but the head of a baby elephant, and people like to give him the goodies that baby elephants love the best.

Ganesh is known as the god who removes obstacles. Many Hindus ask for his blessing before beginning any undertaking, be it something as big as getting married, or something as small as planting a single seed. Ganesh makes wishes come true—if they are good wishes—and helps people find a way around their difficulties.

Ganesh is a friendly little god who is loved as much as he is worshipped. He is appealing, humble, and even comical. Instead of riding on a bird of prey or some monstrous beast, he rides a little mouse. Like Ganesh himself, the lowly, nibbling mouse knows no obstacles. Together they go anywhere they need to.

Hindus see Ganesh as the god who has the power to make all good things happen. He inspires people to love one another, to play beautiful music, paint marvelous pictures, or write really good books. And if anyone is fighting an injustice or struggling with someone who is unfair, that person can depend on Ganesh. With his help, justice prevails, and right wins out over wrong.

You are probably wondering how in the world a little boy wound up with the head of a baby elephant, and what in the world gives him so much power to make things go right. Like Ganesh himself, the story is strange and wonderful. Listen carefully, and I'll tell it to you.

Shiva, God of Destruction, was married to the beautiful mother goddess Parvati, who had come to Earth in the form of a mountain princess. He loved his wife deeply and passionately, but he cared nothing for the schedules or dress codes or manners of a royal household. Clad in a tiger skin, with live serpents coiled around his waist and shoulders, a crescent moon on his brow, and long matted hair down his back, he roamed the wilderness for weeks at a time, with no one but animals for company.

In spite of his unruly ways, Parvati loved Shiva just the way he was. The only time she protested his behavior was when he arrived in her private chambers without warning and interrupted her in her bath.

One afternoon Parvati lay soaking in a warm tub. Shiva had been gone for weeks. When would she see him next? Would he burst through the door right then and there? The thought of him barging in so rudely troubled Parvati and made it hard for her to relax.

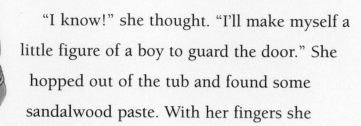

"I know!" she thought. "I'll make myself a little figure of a boy to guard the door." She hopped out of the tub and found some sandalwood paste. With her fingers she fashioned a head, a cute button nose, and two big eyes. Working quickly, she created sturdy legs and arms. The figurine looked quite lifelike!

She took a breath, and blew life into it.

Suddenly, a little boy sprang forth, as strong and handsome as could be. He jumped lightly to the floor and turned to face her.

"Dear Mother," the boy said, "now that I am here, what can I do for you?"

"Dear Son, please just stand at the palace door while I finish my bath, and do not let anyone in." She gave him a slender wand to hold. "Here," she said with a smile. "Just wave this at anyone who tries to enter."

The little boy was proud and pleased. He had no idea that Parvati was a goddess or that the stick in his hand was magic. He was happy just to march back and forth in front of the palace, waving his wand like a baton, prepared to stop anyone who tried to disturb his newfound mother.

And so when Shiva, true to form, strode up to the palace door, he found a sturdy youngster with a strong voice and determined eyes barring his way.

"Entry denied, sir!" said the boy.

Shiva was puzzled. Who was this child? And why was he, Lord Shiva, God of Destruction, experiencing such difficulty getting past him? Shiva found he couldn't take a single step forward! There was some strange, powerful force holding him back. As usual, though, Shiva was in a hurry to return to the forest, so he asked his pet bull, Nandi, to investigate for him.

The bull, backed up by Shiva's helpers, a band of ruffians called
the Shivaganas, lowered his long horns to attack. But the brave little
boy waved his wand, once, twice, three times—and before they knew
it, Nandi and his cohorts were in full retreat. They were mortified.
This was the very first time anyone had dared stand up to them.
And worse yet, they had been defeated by a pudgy little boy!

They found Shiva walking in the forest. "I'm sorry, Lord Shiva,"
Nandi said, hanging his great head in shame. "The boy just waved
his wand! We could not go forward. It must have been very
powerful magic!"

Far away, the sage Narada—an amazing and wise spirit who traveled between Heaven and Earth and the netherworlds below—heard every word. Narada kept careful watch on all goings on in the universe, and he could carry news of events and problems at the speed of light. The way he told the news made everyone pay attention, too! When Narada got involved, you could be sure that things would really start happening.

When he saw the boy drive all intruders from Parvati's door, Narada flew straight off to the heavenly palaces of Brahma and Vishnu. "This child has effortlessly turned away Shiva, his fearsome bull, Nandi, and a battalion of the invincible Shivaganas," he told them. Narada was not one to mince words. "Watch out! What if this little boy grows stronger and stronger? He might turn you all out of Heaven! The whole world will be in turmoil! He could turn the entire universe upside down! You must act now!" Of course, when they heard this, Brahma and Vishnu could not simply sit and wait. They decided to consult with Shiva, and Shiva was happy to accept their help.

Because children in India are taught to respect their elders and politely do whatever they ask, the three gods decided that Brahma should disguise himself as an old professor with a long beard and scholarly robes. He would go to the door where the boy stood guard and try to reason with him. Surely the child would step aside for a kind old teacher.

"My dear young man," said Brahma, "you must put that wand down and let me through at once. Don't be silly, now. I can see you are a well-behaved, smart little boy. Surely you know enough to obey your elders. There is no reason to stand here driving people away. No one will hurt you." Brahma prattled on and on, sweet-talking and gently chiding the boy. But Parvati's son was not to be distracted from his duty. He pounced on the old professor. "I obey only my mother! My mother told me to stand here and to let no one through." He pulled roughly on Brahma's beard. "Entry denied, sir!" he said.

When Brahma reported back to Shiva and Vishnu, Shiva decided that it was time to get tougher with the boy. "I will summon Indra, Lord of the Skies. He and his elephant vehicle move like the wind, and my own son, Kartikeya, commands Indra's army. No one can defeat him. You'll see," Shiva said with confidence. "The boy will soon be gone, sent back to wherever he came from."

So the army gathered. Kartikeya, with a huge arsenal of weapons, rode up on his impressive vehicle, a large and beautiful peacock. Indra, the king of the lesser gods, sat astride his gigantic white elephant. Indra's weapons were nothing less than the tempests themselves—thunder, lightning, rain, and hail. The air crackled with a thousand gathering storms.

On one side of Heaven, the gods nodded in approval.

But Parvati was furious. Here was a horde of ruthless soldiers, aided by the force of hurricanes, amassed against her beloved son, who faced them with only a slender wand and the strength of his courage and determination.

"This is an injustice!" she cried.

Remember that Parvati was a goddess. She could take any form she wished, and when she saw what was happening she changed herself into the fierce Nav Durga, a frightening goddess who could multiply her body over and over again. Thus transformed, she rushed to the boy's aid on the back of a fearsome tiger, shooting arrows and throwing curved daggers while the boy brandished his wand at the oncoming forces. It is Nav Durga's job to protect and defend those in need, and she has never lost a battle. With her support, the little boy won easily. The soldiers fled in terror—even the wind and thunderheads blew away.

Now the gods were really concerned. Narada's words were coming true. Never before had the gods and goddesses battled each other with such bitterness and anger. This boy was more troublesome—and more powerful—than the gods could handle. They must get rid of him!

Vishnu decided to use his ultimate weapon, the razor-sharp chakra that spun on his index finger. He summoned his eagle, Garuda, and flew to where the little boy stood guard. As Vishnu poised his finger to let loose the deadly disc, the boy hurled the full force of his wand. Spinning through the air, Vishnu's chakra sliced the wand in two.

Undaunted, the boy picked up one of the pieces and hurled it at Vishnu again.

"Entry denied, sir!" he cried.

In defense of his master, Garuda caught the wand in his powerful beak. But it had been a close call; the boy could have hurt Vishnu terribly.

Shiva, standing near, was enraged to see the boy attacking Vishnu. This boy was humiliating them all! Shiva rushed forward to help.

18

The boy didn't see Shiva approach. He didn't hear the trident blade slicing through the air. Shiva swung once, and with that single blow cut the little boy's head right off!

Poor Parvati watched in horror. The boy she had created and loved was dead. Her son had acted with unquestioning devotion, defying the most powerful gods to protect her privacy. He had only done as she wished. Now his body lay lifeless on the ground, his head severed dreadfully and damaged beyond repair.

A mother's grief is a most powerful force, and Parvati's anguish was equaled by an implacable anger. The sound of her cries shook the heavens, and the terrifying form of the goddess Kali sprang from her forehead. A host of other goddesses joined her, vowing to avenge the child. They rampaged like a whirlwind, laying waste to anything or anyone that stood in their way. They showed no mercy.

In desperation, Brahma and Vishnu appealed to Parvati. "You are destroying everything! Heaven will be ripped to pieces; the earth will spin off its axis. Please, we beg you, calm down."

She stared at them, eyes blazing. "You killed my son. This is *your* doing. If you want to preserve the balance between Heaven and Earth, then you must bring my son back to life."

At last the gods understood. "Parvati," said Vishnu, "we have wronged you. We will give your little boy back to you. I will search the earth and find a suitable head for him, and he will be whole once again."

And so Lord Vishnu crossed over the land, back and forth, searching for just the right creature who could donate its head to bring the boy back to life. "Too placid . . . too furry . . . too jumpy . . . too noisy . . . too scary," he muttered to himself as he passed by cows and goats, rabbits and donkeys, cats and dogs, tigers and wolves. He wanted to give the boy the strength and wisdom of the best possible animal. Finally he came upon a baby elephant, lying back to back with its mother. "Perfect!" Vishnu thought, and he woke up the baby's mother.

"Mother elephant," he told her, "there is a terrible war being waged in Heaven and on Earth. If you would spare your son, I believe we can restore order in the universe."

The mother elephant was very sad to give up her baby, but she

agreed. "When Brahma created us elephants," she said, "he gave us many valuable qualities: loyalty, strength, keen senses, long memories, calm minds, and great wisdom. I know my son will serve you well."

She stroked her baby gently with her trunk. "May you have a long and happy life," she murmured. "I will never forget you."

"Don't worry," said Vishnu. "Your son will be immortal now. No one will ever forget him." As he touched the little elephant, he passed on to the baby animal all of his love and compassion. Then he used his chakra to remove the little elephant's head, which he carried back to where the little boy's body lay.

Brahma took the head from Vishnu and placed it on the body of the little boy. As he did so, he also passed on to the child all of his own wisdom and resourcefulness. Parvati was overjoyed to see her son stretch his limbs as he slowly came back to life. She thought he looked perfect and didn't mind at all that he was different than before.

Her little boy settled happily in her lap. She put her arm around him and said, "Welcome back."

Shiva leaned forward and placed his hand on the little boy's head, blessing this new addition to the family and passing on his kindness and immense energy. "Your mother, Parvati, is my wife," he said, "so I adopt you as my son. From now on, you may call me Father."

Everyone rejoiced to see the end of the war and bloodshed. Far away, Narada watched and listened and smiled his approval.

As it happened, while Parvati and Shiva and all the other gods and goddesses were busy fighting over the boy who guarded Parvati's door, the people on Earth had been having some troubles of their own. Many of their problems were caused by Shiva's assistants, the Shivaganas, who enjoyed stirring up trouble, just for the fun of it. They loved to create confusion and arguments and delays, and lately they'd been running wild while Shiva's attention was elsewhere. The people grew more and more miserable as their problems multiplied.

There was no one in Heaven who could help them. Lord Brahma was too busy creating everything in the world. Lord Vishnu was responsible for keeping Brahma's creations healthy and prosperous. And it was Shiva's job to clear out space for new creations, so the world would not get too crowded. They had no time to help mere mortals with day-to-day questions and problems.

But now Brahma looked down from Heaven to see his creation in chaos and realized the people on Earth needed a god of their own, a friendly god who could help them with their everyday problems. They especially needed someone who could get Shiva's attention and remind him to discipline the Shivaganas when they got out of hand.

Brahma and Vishnu thought that one of Shiva's own sons would be ideal for the job. But they didn't know which son would be the better choice. It would be a job that required intelligence and resourcefulness and, most of all, wisdom.

So the gods arranged a contest between the elephant-headed boy and Shiva and Parvati's first son, Kartikeya, to see who had those qualities in greatest measure.

"This is a race," Vishnu said. He pointed to Shiva and Parvati, who sat together on a hilltop. "The starting place is at your parents' side. You need to circle the whole universe. Whoever returns first will be chosen as Shiva's representative and will lead the Shivaganas on Earth."

26

Kartikeya brushed his robes and showed off his weapons. Privately, he thought he and his speedy peacock would win the race. When the elephant-headed boy appeared—riding a little mouse—Kartikeya couldn't help laughing.

"You won't get far on *that!*" he said.

With much saber rattling and feather shaking, Kartikeya and the peacock soared off on their long, long journey around the universe. "I'll be back," he called, his voice fading in the distance. Then the little boy calmly hopped upon his mouse. He had chosen the unassuming mouse as his vehicle for a very good reason—the lowly mouse always manages to get anywhere it wants to go.

"Here I go," said the boy with a humble bow to everyone. He circled once around Parvati and Shiva, and then he bowed again. His mouse bowed too. "I'm back," he said.

The gods stared. "What do you think you're doing?" they asked.

"I have completed my journey," the boy explained patiently. "You, mother and father, are everything to me. You have given me life, just as the sun and the earth give energy to all living beings. So, I love and respect you as much as I love and respect Heaven, Sun, and Earth. When I circle around you, I circle my entire universe."

"You speak wisely," said Brahma. "You show intelligence, clarity, loyalty, and insight. We hereby give you the name Ganesh, which means leader of the Shivaganas. Your job is to help people on Earth whenever they're in trouble or in need."

To this day, the immortal elephant-headed Ganesh lives in temples, shrines, and homes all over India, helping people overcome all the obstacles that life puts before them. With love and devotion, they start each day by praying to Ganesh and seeking his blessings.

Note to Parents and Teachers

Stories from the ancient past are full of wisdom and enduring truths that continue to be relevant today. The story of Ganesh is essentially a story of a child's devotion and loyalty to his mother and of that mother's love for her child. The minute Ganesh jumps from Parvati's palm he is ready to do whatever he can to serve her, and he doesn't let anything sway him from his determined course. He bravely stands firm in the face of raging bulls, roaring hurricanes, and entire armies. It helps to have a magic wand, of course, but nevertheless, Ganesh serves as a model for modern children of someone who sticks to his principles. A child with Ganesh's strength of character wouldn't let himself be pushed around by peer pressure or the mass media once he'd set his mind on a fair cause worth defending.

Parvati, for her part, loves her child no matter what. When she feels that he has been wronged, she does everything in her power to defend him. And when Shiva commits the unforgivable act of beheading him, Parvati's grief and anger know no bounds. Because she is a goddess, her rage touches off a cosmic battle between the entire pantheon of Hindu goddesses and gods. As in all mythological stories, it is a symbolic battle, and what is at stake is the entire balance of the universe. Indian mythology gives equal value to the forces of creation and the forces of destruction—the important thing is to keep those forces in equilibrium. When he restores Ganesh to life with the head of the baby elephant, Brahma keeps the forces of destruction from spinning entirely out of control.

And Parvati, good mother that she is, loves her child as much as she ever did. His strange appearance doesn't matter to her at all. Parvati's unwavering love reminds parents that all children need unconditional love, no matter how they look or what skills and abilites they possess. By loving children fully, parents ensure the future of humanity. In today's world, where so many forces conspire to undermine the strength of the family, it is reassuring for children and parents alike to discover stories that confirm that an outpouring of energy in the form of love, loyalty, and devotion can bring families together, healing society one family at a time.

About the Illustrations

The original illustrations for *How Ganesh Got His Elephant Head* are wash paintings done in both watercolors and opaque tempera paints. The artist created each piece following a nine-step traditional Indian process.

1. First, using watercolors, he drew the outlines of everything in the painting.

2. Before filling in the outlines he had to "fix" the line drawing, pouring water over the painted surface until only the paint absorbed by the paper remained.

3. Once the paper was completely dry, he filled in all the forms with color, using three tones for each color to achieve a three-dimensional effect: highlight, middle tone, and depth.

4. Once again the colors had to be fixed by pouring water over the painting until the water ran off clear.

5. Then, still using watercolor, he applied the background colors.

6. Once again the colors had to be fixed.

7. Then the artist was ready to apply the wash, which is done with opaque tempera paints mixed to a consistency between thin honey and boiled milk. Before applying the wash, he had to wet the painting thoroughly, letting any excess water drip off. Then he applied the tempera paint until the whole painting appeared to be behind a colored fog. While the wash color was still wet, he took a dry brush and removed it from the face, hands, and feet of any figures. Then he let the wash dry completely.

8. Once again water had to be poured over the entire painting to fix the color. Many of the paintings received several washes and fixes before the right color tone was achieved. The wash color is important because it sets the emotional mood of the entire painting.

9. Finally, the artist went back in and redefined the delicate line work of the piece, outlining faces, fingers, toes, and ornaments with the depth color. These finishing touches allow the painting to reemerge from within the clouds of wash.

To give children an opportunity for hands-on participation in this ancient art form, we have included a line drawing of Ganesh on the following page. Feel free to trace or photocopy the image so that children may color it in.